WANT TO BE A KNIGHT?

Paul Mason

Crabtree Publishing Company
www.crabtreebooks.com

Author: Paul Mason
Editors: Kathy Middleton
Crystal Sikkens
Project coordinator: Kathy Middleton
Production coordinator: Ken Wright
Prepress technicians: Ken Wright
Margaret Amy Salter

Picture Credits:
Dreamstime: Aliced: page 13; Diademimages: page 21; Iakov Filimonov: page 10; Sergey Khruschov: page 16; Ints Vikamanis: pages 1, 8
Photolibrary: The British Library: page 20
Shutterstock: cover; Isa Ismail: page 9; Litvin Leonid: page 5; Jose Marines: pages 3, 6; Muránsky: page 17; Nichola Piccillo: page 14; Puchan: page 11; Raulin: pages 7, 12; Topal: page 18; Makarova Viktoria: page 15; Darja Vorontsova: page 19; Elena Yakusheva: page 4

Library and Archives Canada Cataloguing in Publication

Mason, Paul, 1967-
    Want to be a knight? / Paul Mason.

(Crabtree connections)
Includes index.
ISBN 978-0-7787-7845-5 (bound).--ISBN 978-0-7787-7867-7 (pbk.)

    1. Knights and knighthood--Europe--History--Juvenile literature. 2. Civilization, Medieval--Juvenile literature. I. Title. II. Series: Crabtree connections

CR4513.M383 2011   j940.1   C2011-900608-1

Library of Congress Cataloging-in-Publication Data

Mason, Paul, 1967-
    Want to be a knight? / Paul Mason.
        p. cm. -- (Crabtree connections)
    Includes index.
    ISBN 978-0-7787-7867-7 (pbk. : alk. paper) -- ISBN 978-0-7787-7845-5 (reinforced library binding : alk. paper)
    1. Knights and knighthood--Europe--History--Juvenile literature. 2. Civilization, Medieval--Juvenile literature. I. Title. II. Series.

CR4513.M383 2012
940.1--dc22

2011001347

Printed in the U.S.A./072011/WO20110114

Published in Canada
Crabtree Publishing
616 Welland Ave.
St. Catharines, Ontario
L2M 5V6

Published in the United States
Crabtree Publishing
PMB 59051
350 Fifth Avenue, 59th Floor
New York, New York 10118

Contents

A Knight's World

Long ago when knights were alive, life was not much fun for most people. There were a lot of wars, a lot of disease, and not a lot to eat.

A knight's life

It was a different story for knights. Knights got all the good food and lived in **castles**! Of course, everyone wanted to be a knight.

Knights wore helmets for protection.

A tough job

Read on to find out what it took to be a knight. Then decide if you still want to be one.

helmet ——o

Born a Knight

Only boys who come from very important and very **wealthy** families can become knights.

From father to son

Most boys become knights because their fathers are knights. They have to pass many tests first, though.

Knights get to live in amazing castles. Cool!

servant

Help on hand

Knights have a lot of **servants** who look after them and their horses.

Getting Started

A boy who wants to become a knight must leave home when he is seven years old. He goes to work for a **lord**.

Is it hard work?

A boy training to be a knight is called a **page**. He must do a lot of different jobs for his lord.

sword

Pages learn how to fight, too.

toilet

This job stinks!

Pages do some really horrible jobs (that no one else wants to do), such as cleaning the toilet. Gross!

Good Enough?

A page must be a good fighter by the time he is fourteen. If he isn't up to scratch by then, he is sent back home.

What if he makes it?

If a page is allowed to carry on with his training, he becomes a **squire**. Then he works for a knight.

armor

A squire's job includes cleaning a lot of **armor**!

squire

Into battle!

Life as a squire is dangerous, because a squire must always serve his knight even in battle.

Weapons

A squire must look after his knight's armor, shields, and weapons. This is one of his most important jobs.

Why are weapons important?

A knight's life depends on all his weapons working well, so it is important that his squire takes care of them.

Swords must be kept really, really sharp!

flail

War tools

A knight's weapons include **lances**, swords, axes, **maces**, and **flails**. He uses them to bash, mash, and smash!

Warhorses

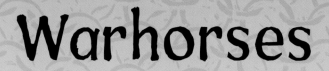

Another job of a squire is to look after his knight's warhorse. A warhorse is a really tough battle horse.

Are warhorses brave?

A warhorse is specially trained for battle, so it will still **charge** even if arrows are flying through the air.

 A warhorse can squash enemies into the ground.

Rich man's ride!

Keeping a warhorse costs a lot of money because they must be fed a lot of hay and oats.

Knight Rules

There are a lot of rules about how a knight must behave. Knights must stick to them carefully.

Knights must never, ever...

- Cheat or lie. No one will trust a knight who does not tell the truth.
- Run away in battle. A knight must be brave so his soldiers will follow him.

Ordinary soldiers are killed and not taken prisoner.

Caught in battle

Knights are taken prisoner in battle. A **ransom** is then paid to free them.

War Practice

Knights practice for war by fighting each other at great **tournaments**. Usually, two knights fight each other to win a prize.

Does a squire fight too?

A squire helps his knight with his armor and weapons, but he does not fight until he is a knight.

Hello, ladies!

Knights fight for more than money —they also hope to **impress** ladies!

Knights sometimes fight on foot.

Made It!

A squire is often killed in battle. But if he lives to be twenty-one, he may finally become a knight.

How is a squire made a knight?

A squire is made a knight by his king. The king touches him on his shoulders and says, "Arise, Sir Knight!" From that moment on, he is a knight.

A squire becomes a knight.

king

Don't relax yet

No one wants to end up as a skeleton. However, if a knight isn't killed in battle, he will probably die young anyway from disease.

Glossary

armor Metal suit worn to protect the body in battle

castles Huge stone buildings in which knights lived

charge To rush ahead into battle

flails Heavy clubs with chains and spiked balls

impress To make someone think you are great

lances Long, spear-like weapons

lord Important man who had a large house or castle

maces Long clubs with heavy weights on the end

page A boy training to be a knight

ransom Money paid to free someone who has been captured

servants People whose jobs are to do whatever they are told by someone who is in charge of them

squire A knight's personal servant

tournaments Fights in which knights test their skills

wealthy To have a lot of money

Further Reading

Web Sites

Find out more about how people became knights at:
www.middle-ages.org.uk/steps-to-knighthood.htm

Find out what kinds of competitions took place at jousts and tournaments in medieval times at:
http://medievaleurope.mrdonn.org/jousts.html

Take part in a fun jousting game and learn about weapons, armor, and coats of arms along the way at:
www.tudorbritain.org/joust/

Books

Knight: A Noble Guide for Young Squires by Geoffrey de Lance, Candlewick Press (2006).

The Life of a Knight (The Medieval World) by Kay Eastwood, Crabtree Publishing Company (2004).

Castle and Knight (Eye Wonder), DK Children (2005).

Index